Albertine, Goose Queen

Michael Morpurgo
and Shoo Rayner

Young Lions

First published by A & C Black (Publishers) Limited 1989
Published in Young Lions 1990
20 19 18 17 16 15 14 13 12 11

Young Lions is an imprint of
the Children's Division, part of
HarperCollins*Publishers* Ltd,
77–85 Fulham Palace Road,
Hammersmith, London W6 8JB

Text copyright © 1989 Michael Morpurgo
Illustrations copyright © 1989 Shoo Rayner
All rights reserved.

Printed and bound in Great Britain by Clays Ltd, St Ives plc

Chapter One

There was once a family of all sorts
of animals that lived in the
farmyard behind the tumble-down
barn on Mudpuddle Farm.

cock-a-doodle-doo-be-doobie-doobie-doobie

At first light every morning
Frederick, the flame-feathered
cockerel, lifted his eyes to the sun and
crowed and crowed until the light
came on in old Farmer Rafferty's
bedroom window.

One by one the animals crept out into the dawn and stretched and yawned and scratched themselves.

oh, what a beautiful day!

But no-one ever spoke a word, not
until after breakfast.

Chapter Two

One morning, just after breakfast,
old Farmer Rafferty brought
Captain, the great black carthorse,
in from his field and led him into his
stable in the corner of the yard.

I'm shutting you in here, Captain. The hunt will likely be coming this way today and I don't want you galloping out after them. I'm shutting Jigger in the house as well, otherwise he'll be running off with the hounds. I'll let you both out after they've gone.

And old Farmer Rafferty went out, bolting the stable door behind him.

Captain pricked up his ears. In the
distance he could hear the hunting
horn and the baying of the foxhounds.

10

Soon all the animals in the
farmyard had heard it too and
were running for cover.

Here they come! You'd better get inside, all of you. They'll chase anything that moves.

Peggoty rounded up her little pigs (not forgetting Pintsize, the littlest of them all.)

Auntie Grace and Primrose, the two dreamy-eyed cows, made off towards the barn door as fast as they could go.

While Auntie Grace and Primrose were agreeing, Egbert, the greedy goat, Diana, the silly sheep, and Frederick, the flame-feathered cockerel, ran past them into the safety of the barn.

Aunty Grace and Primrose both decided to go in at the same time.

But Albertine the white goose
stayed just where she was, sitting
serenely on her island in the pond.

Howl Yap Woof Ya

What a fuss.

Upside and Down, the two white
ducks that no one could tell apart,
were upside-down in the water so
they couldn't see or hear
what was going on.

HUBBLE
BUBBLE

GLOOP
GLOOP

And Mossop, who had been fast asleep on the tractor seat, shinned up the tallest lime tree and hissed with terrible fury. He hated being woken up.

Chapter Three

The hounds came through the gate.
They came over the gate and round
the gate, noses glued to the ground,
tails swishing in the air.

Behind them came red-coated,
red-faced huntsmen on snorting
horses that tossed their heads
and flashed their eyes.

And the hunt clattered through the yard and away.

Farmer Rafferty went in to shave.
He only shaved when he remembered
to, and he remembered to now.

Chapter Four

The animals crept out of the barn
and into the bright sunlight of the
yard. They did not notice the
panting pink tongue nor the pricked
up ears of the fox as he crawled
out of a bramble hedge smiling his
sneaky smile.

Here we go!

But Albertine did.

'Good morning, dear friends,'
he said in his sneaky voice.

And all the animals jumped in their
skins and clung to each other in fear
and trembling.

Don't be frightened, dear friends.
I ask you, do I look as
if I'd hurt a hair on your head or a
feather on your back?
It's a hard life being a fox.
Not a friend in the world. No one to
talk to. No one to play with.

He sighed a sad and sneaky sigh.
Then he cast a long and horrible
sneaky look across the pond at
Albertine.

The animals hid behind each other
and kept their distance. Only
Pintsize was brave enough to
step forward.

I'll play with you. I can chase my
own tail and catch it quick as a twick,
so I can easily catch you.

But Peggoty picked little Pintsize
up by his ear and dropped him
under Aunty Grace's legs with all
her other little pigs.

The fox wiped a sneaky tear from his eye.

Back home in my den, I have a wife and five little babies, all of them starving to death because I can't find any food to take home to them. Without food my babies will die. Won't you help me, dear friends? I beg you, think of my babies.

And all the animals thought of his babies and they could scarcely hold back their tears.

'A fox is a fox is a fox,' said Albertine wisely from her island on the pond. But no one was listening to her.

Poor thing.

said Aunty Grace.

It's a crying shame.

agreed Primrose.

Babies, seventy-five of them I've had in my life – seventy-six if you count Pintsize. I've had more babies than you've had hot dinners – all the world to me they are; so I understand how you feel. We'll help you feed your babies, won't we?

And they all agreed they would.

From his stable Captain could just see what was going and he whinnied his warning.

The animals thought he was calling after the huntsmen's horses – but he wasn't.

Jigger, the always sensible sheepdog,
could smell the rank smell of fox
and barked loudly from inside old
Farmer Rafferty's house.

The animals thought he was calling
after the huntsmen's hounds — but
he wasn't.

'You are so kind, dear friends,' said the fox smiling his sneaky smile. 'I don't need much. Just some milk, a few eggs, barley, wheat, oats, anything you can find. And there's no need to hurry back. Take your time.'

So one by one the animals left the yard until only Albertine was left sitting on her island.

And Mossop of Course...

Don't forget the old Mossop who was watching everything from his branch high up in the lime tree.

And be sure you don't forget the sneaky fox who was padding slowly towards the pond, his tail whisking to and fro, his tongue sharpening his teeth.

Chapter Five

Mossop watched in horror from his branch as the fox tested the water with his front paw,  shook it,

SHAKE

then slid slowly into the water

and swam out across the pond towards Albertine.

Who sat still as a statue.

Once on the island the fox shook
himself dry and licked his lips.

But Albertine sat serene and still
and looked down her nose at the fox
as he came creeping towards her.

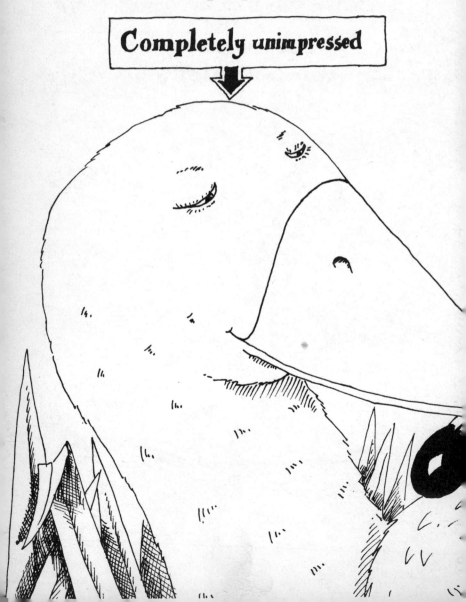

41

'Mr Fox,' said Albertine, 'I am not
afraid to die. All of us have to die.
All of us have to die one day, you
know. Even you, Mr Fox. You can eat
me, but please, Mr Fox, take pity
on my children. Let them live.

I'm trying to
eat her and
she's making
speeches!

They did not see Mossop letting himself down the lime tree and scampering across the farmyard to fetch help!

Mossop to the rescue!

As Albertine spoke, she stood up
and three yellow goslings ran out
from under her feathers.

44

Chapter Six

The fox jumped back in surprise.

'You are brave, Madam,' he said in
a voice that was suddenly gentle
and kind, and not at all sneaky.

47

Five of the little perishers, and they never stop eating. You have three lovely children, Madam, and they have a brave mother. No, I just can't do it. I can't kill you or your babies. Oh dear, and I was so looking forward to a nice fat goose - begging your pardon.

At that very moment the hunting horn sounded. TARAN-TARA-

Chapter Seven

There was a terrible baying of
hounds across the fields and the
drumming of horses' hooves.
The hunt was coming back . . .

The fox looked around him on the
island, but there was nowhere to
hide. It would take too long to swim
across the pond and he knew it.
He looked at Albertine with
pleading eyes.

Won't you help me?
I beg you,
please help me.

TARAN·TARA·TARAN·

'He's got to be here somewhere,'
said the huntsman with the
ginger beard.

YAROO·WO·WO·WOOOF

And they all roared with laughter
and galloped off past the pond
and away.

But if the red-faced, red-coated
huntsmen had been in less of a
hurry they would have noticed that
the goose had suddenly grown

a long, red, bushy Tail!

Chapter Eight

By the time Mossop came running back into the yard with the animals behind him, they found Albertine sitting quite alone on her island.

'Where is she?' asked Egbert, the greedy goat, practising his butting. 'I'll get him, I'll get that fox.'

This tale's not over yet!

Even Auntie Grace (who was
hardly ever angry) was lowering
her head and pawing the ground
like a bull.

And so, of course, Primrose did
the same.

And Mossop hissed
out his fury at
the edge of
the pond.

'I'm in here,' said the fox, as he crawled out from under Albertine's feathers, followed by three fluffy yellow goslings.

Well, one good turn does deserve another. He could have killed me and my little ones; but he took pity on us. Who would have thought it of a fox?

'Not me,' said the fox, shaking his head. 'Don't know what came over me. I'd better go before I change my mind.'

And he swam back across the pond and vanished over the hedge.

Chapter Nine

Later that afternoon

Upside

and Down

at last

lifted
their
heads

out of the water.

'Had a good day?' Albertine enquired kindly, settled once again on her goslings.

'S'pose you've been sitting there all day doing nothing?' Upside sniggered, or was it Down - no one could tell the difference.

'You could say that,' Albertine said.

'Silly old goose,' said Upside, or Down, and they both turned upside-down again.

The night came down, the moon
came up, and everyone slept on
Mudpuddle Farm.